It's a Deal,
DOGBOY

For my son, Doo Wook,
with pride, gratitude, and love
—C. M.

VIKING
Published by the Penguin Group
Penguin Putnam Books for Young Readers, 345 Hudson Street, New York, New York 10014, U.S.A.
Penguin Books Ltd, 27 Wrights Lane, London W8 5TZ, England
Penguin Books Australia Ltd, Ringwood, Victoria, Australia
Penguin Books Canada Ltd, 10 Alcorn Avenue, Toronto, Ontario, Canada M4V 3B2
Penguin Books (N.Z.) Ltd, 182-190 Wairau Road, Auckland 10, New Zealand

Penguin Books Ltd, Registered Offices: Harmondsworth, Middlesex, England

First published in 1998 by Viking, a member of Penguin Putnam Books for Young Readers.

3 5 7 9 10 8 6 4 2

Text copyright © Christine McDonnell, 1998
Illustrations copyright © G. Brian Karas, 1998

LIBRARY OF CONGRESS CATALOGING-IN-PUBLICATION DATA
McDonnell, Christine.
It's a deal, Dogboy / by Christine McDonnell.   p.   cm.
Summary: During the summer between third and fourth grades, Leo plays in a baseball league, buys
his sister's tree house and camps out in it with his friend Johnny, gets a dog from the animal shelter,
and endures a visit from his whining younger cousin Tim.
ISBN 0-670-83264-2
[1. Baseball—Fiction. 2. Tree house—Fiction.
3. Dogs—Fiction. 4. Cousins—Fiction.] I. Title.
PZ7.M47843It 1998 [Fic]—DC21 98-3845 CIP AC

Printed in U.S.A.   Set in Fairfield

It's a Deal,
DOGBOY

by Christine McDonnell
illustrated by
G. Brian Karas

VIKING

Pranks

"**S**ummerti-i-i-i-ime," the voices on the oldies station crooned. Leo groaned, until he remembered what day it was. He sat straight up in bed, knocking the cat off onto the floor. With a squeaky protest, she padded out with her tail in the air.

Downstairs, Leo found his mother in the backyard watering her plants. The air was already muggy. "Last day of school," he crowed.

"It's going to be a scorcher," Mrs. Nolan said. "There's fruit in the refrigerator. I'll be in as soon as I give these guys a drink." She talked about her plants as if they were people.

Leo's sister, Eleanor, sat at the kitchen table reading the sports section of the newspaper. She was eating grapes one by one. "Bet I can fit more grapes in my mouth than you," Leo challenged.

"Get your own fruit, Dogboy," Eleanor said without taking her eyes away from the newspaper.

Even Eleanor couldn't dampen Leo's happiness. "Free at last. Free at last," Leo said. "Tomorrow I'm going to sleep late, watch cartoons, do nothing."

"Unless you have to go to summer school," Eleanor said.

There were no more grapes in the refrigerator. He settled for strawberries. Summer school. Those two words didn't belong together. "They don't have summer school for my grade," Leo said.

"So instead of summer school, you'll have to repeat. Wow, Leo, another year with Miss Wiltshire!" Eleanor teased.

Before Leo could answer, his mother came in from the garden and dried her hands on a striped dishcloth. "The garage has got to be cleaned and the cellar needs sorting. It's like a junkyard. I need you both tomorrow."

"Oh, Mo-om," Eleanor whined. "I'm going swimming tomorrow with Nancy and Joan."

"Help with the cellar first, then wash off the dust at the lake. I'll even drive you." This was a rare offer; she usually made them ride their bikes. "You, too, Leo."

"I don't want *him* tagging along with us," Eleanor said.

"Promise me you won't fight all summer," Mrs. Nolan said. "I may have to resort to earplugs and sign language."

Leo rolled his tongue inside out and crossed his eyes at his sister. "Who wants to be with you? I'm going with Johnny," he said.

"Great," Eleanor said, rolling her eyes. "Two of you."

Hearing Johnny's whistle, Leo said, "Half day today, Mom. I don't need lunch." He kissed the air by her ear.

"Bring your report card straight home," Mrs. Nolan said. "Don't lose it, Leo."

"She wants to see if you're promoted to fourth grade," Eleanor teased.

Leo wheeled his bike down the driveway. Promoted? He'd never thought about it. Another year in Miss Wiltshire's class? Wilty wouldn't want him around for another year, he told himself. Still, Eleanor's words made him uneasy.

Leo and Johnny always followed the same route to school: along the river, over the stone bridge, and five blocks up North Street. They reversed it on the way home, adding a stop at Patsy's Bakery or the pizza shop.

"What do you think we'll do today?" Johnny asked.

"Wash desks. Take stuff down. All that end-of-the-year junk."

"Maybe Miss Wiltshire will bring a treat." Johnny sounded hopeful.

"Wilty bring us food? She never gave us anything all year."

"Sure she did. Remember the bookmarks?" Johnny said.

"Right. Cardboard strips with stickers." Leo swung his arm as if he was twirling a lasso over his head. "Whoopee! If Wilty brings food, it'll be stale saltines and watery Kool-Aid. The blue kind."

At the playground they locked their bikes to the fence and sat in the shade until the whistle blew. "Bet you fifty cents there's food," Johnny said.

"You're wasting your money," Leo said. "It's a deal."

Miss Wiltshire waited at the classroom door, smiling. She wore an apron over her dress. Johnny poked Leo in the side. "She's been baking good-bye cupcakes and forgot to take it off," he whispered. Leo read the list on the board: *1. Wash your desk inside and out. 2. Sign up for a cleaning job.* Miss Wiltshire's apron was for cleaning, not cooking.

"As soon as we've finished our clean-up, we'll go out for recess, and then it will be time for the end-of-the-year assembly," Miss Wiltshire told the class.

Leo raised his hand. "When do we get our report cards?"

"At the assembly, just before dismissal." Miss Wiltshire winked at Leo.

Why did she wink? he wondered. Maybe it's a hint. But was it good or bad?

"Let's get started, everyone," Miss Wiltshire said. "Desks first."

"Maybe there'll be a snack at recess," Johnny said as he and Leo filled a bucket at the sink.

"You've got food on the brain. Get another sponge. I've got the cleanser."

Johnny looked inside his empty desk. "I hate cleaning old gum."

"At least it's yours. Gum under the project table could be anyone's," Leo said. "Hurry so we can sign up for a job. Anything but the project table."

Johnny nodded. "How about the chalkboards?"

Leo looked around the room for ideas. Ivy and Emily were already taking the colored paper off the bulletin board. "How did they finish their desks so fast?" Leo said. "If we get the chalkboards, we can clap erasers, too."

Leo finished first because he didn't have any gum to scrape. Johnny had at least twelve pastel-colored lumps stuck inside and under his desk. "Look at all that waste," he said in disgust.

"I'll start on the boards," Leo said. "Hurry up, okay?"

Johnny nodded and accidentally bumped his head against the bottom of his desk.

Leo liked washing the boards. He had his own technique. He started by drawing wet zigzags all over the dusty black surface. Then he rinsed the sponge and carefully, stroke after stroke, made even, wet stripes from the top to the bottom covering the surface completely. He was so careful that the first wet stripes were disappearing by the time he reached the end of the board.

Miss Wiltshire sat at her desk stapling reading lists. "Thank you, Leo. You always do such a nice job." She gave him a big smile. Was this another sign? Leo wondered. Maybe she wants me around to wash her boards next year, too. Leo looked over at Miss Wiltshire again. She reminded him of a doll Eleanor had saved from when she was younger. He stared more closely. How could he not have noticed sooner? Miss Wiltshire looked just like Baby Bess, with her big round face and wide-open blue eyes! Her hair was the same, too, stiff brown curls and ridges all close to her head, shiny as plastic. She had baby-doll hands, too, Leo realized, with dimples for knuckles and creases on her wrists.

Leo told Johnny when they were outside clapping erasers. "She looks exactly like a giant Baby Bess."

"Think she wets as soon as she drinks anything?" Johnny joked.

"That's Betsy Wetsy. Baby Bess cries when you push the button on her back. She stops when you rock her."

"Wilty doesn't cry," Johnny said.

"You never found the button on her back."

Leo stamped the wall with an eraser, leaving a chalky L on the bricks.

"Do you think we'll get promoted?" Leo asked Johnny.

"Sure. Why not?"

Leo shrugged. He thought of all the worksheets he hadn't finished, all the homework he'd forgotten or lost. How could Johnny be so sure? Maybe he'd done all his work.

Hot sun beat against the brick wall, reminding Leo of the lake. "Want to go swimming tomorrow? My mom said she'd drive us to the lake."

Johnny wiped his face with the bottom of his T-shirt. "Sure." He finished the capital J and started on R for Ringer. "Maybe we'll come back in the fall and these letters will still be here. J. R. and L. N."

Leo and Johnny had just finished stamping a border around their initials when the class trickled outside for mid-morning break. It was too hot to run. Heat rose up off the asphalt in shimmery bands. Some girls folded paper fans and sat under the trees waving them back and forth like old-fashioned ladies. Ignoring the heat, Ivy practiced with her juggling sticks. Leo watched. Ivy kept her eyes on the sticks and bit her lip in concentration.

"It's hard, huh?" Leo said.

Ivy nodded.

"Think I could learn?"

Ivy nodded again, frowning as she tried to keep the stick in the air.

"Will you teach me?" Leo asked.

The stick hit the ground with a thud. Ivy glared at Leo, a hand on each hip.

"What did I do?" Leo protested. "I was just watching."

"Watch and don't talk."

Leo couldn't watch without talking, so he headed toward the swings. He pumped halfheartedly. It was so hot that even the air blowing past his face didn't feel cool.

Johnny came running up. He opened his hand to show a green balloon. "The first grade had a party. They dropped this."

"So?" Leo was too hot to care.

"Balloon. Water fountain. Water balloon." Johnny grinned. "Water balloon. Girls. Get it? The perfect way to end the year. Wilty will never forget us."

This worried Leo. If he didn't get promoted and Wilty was his teacher again, she'd remember the water balloon prank. She would, that is, if she ever found out who threw it. "It would be even funnier if we torpedoed the girls and they never knew who did it," he said. "We can hide behind the fire escape and toss it."

Johnny nodded. "Cover me while I fill it up."

The balloon looked like a string bean, long and thin, the hardest kind to fill. Water spurted up, spraying Johnny in the face and wetting his shirt.

"Hurry!" Leo whispered.

Finally Johnny managed to fit the rim of the balloon over the jet, and water bubbled in, expanding it like a giant cucumber. Johnny tied a knot in the end, slipped it under his T-shirt, and cradled it in his arms.

Leo led the way. They ran to the side of the building and dodged behind the fire escape across from the tree where the girls sat fanning themselves.

"No sign of Wilty. Let it fly," Leo said.

Johnny tossed the balloon in a high arc. It landed on the pavement. *Splat!* The balloon burst just as they planned, spraying the group. Girls shrieked and jumped up, shaking the water off their shirts and wiping their faces. "Who did that?" someone demanded. "We're telling," another voice yelled.

Running quickly, Leo and Johnny circled the building. "How can they tell if they don't know who did it?" Leo whispered.

"They can't. Why are you so worried?" Johnny asked.

Leo didn't answer. He didn't want to tell Johnny that he was afraid he might not be promoted.

They entered the playground at the other end and strolled across, hands in their pockets. The girls were fussing like a flock of hens after a fox has made his escape. Leo and Johnny sat on the swings again, enjoying the commotion.

Then Miss Wiltshire appeared with a tray in her

hands. "Surprise, boys and girls," she called. "A celebration. You all deserve it."

"Mouse muffins," Leo whispered, jabbing Johnny's
side.

They stood on tiptoe to see over the heads of the
class crowding around the tray.

"I win!" said Johnny. He clapped his hands over his
head. "I win, I win."

The tray was filled with brownies—not just the
regular baked-from-a-mix brownies cut small to make
a package feed the whole class, but Chocolate Fudge
Delights from Patsy's Bakery.

"Lucky, lucky, lucky," Johnny sang. "Oh lucky me.
Chocolate Fudge Delights and fifty cents."

Johnny's grin was so wide and happy that even Leo
had to smile. He knew Johnny would buy candy and
share it anyway. He took one of the giant brownies
from the tray and sat down on the swing to enjoy it.
After a few bites, Leo's mouth had a grainy sugar feel,
and he was thirsty for plain, cold water. He had at least
three bites left. It tasted so good but his stomach
groaned with heavy frosting and chocolate. "I can't finish it," he sighed.

Johnny agreed. "I can't believe I'm throwing away
good food."

"Let's give it to the ants." Leo pointed to the
mounds clustered by the roots of the maple tree,

where busy ants crawled back and forth, in and out of the anthills, carrying leaf bits and tiny grains of dirt. "They work hard. They deserve a celebration." He put his brownie down on the ground, careful not to bury any ants underneath it. Quickly the ants crawled up the sides, over the icing and down again, lugging away crumbs as large as their bodies.

Johnny set his on the ground near Leo's and the ants swarmed over it. "They match the icing," he said. "If you didn't know they were there, you'd never notice them." Then, with a grin that Leo knew well, Johnny picked up his brownie and sauntered toward the flock of girls fanning themselves in the shade. "Anyone want the rest of my Chocolate Fudge Delight? Charlotte, how about you?" He offered the brownie to a girl who held her nose in the air as if everyone else smelled funny. She was still damp from the water balloon explosion.

She eyed him suspiciously, with eyebrows raised. He tilted his head and smiled an innocent smile.

"I'll take it," Ivy called from the other side of the tree. "Bring it over here, Ringer."

Johnny stretched out his hand toward Charlotte. She patted her pink ballerina barrettes. "Here, Charlotte. It's to make up for teasing you this year," Johnny fibbed.

Leo watched. Would Charlotte take the bait? How could Johnny keep from laughing?

She reached out her hand as if doing Johnny the biggest favor in the world. Then, with a superior smile she popped the brownie into her mouth.

Johnny kept still, eyes fixed on Charlotte's face. Leo began to laugh. He tried to hold it in and choked with the effort. Charlotte kept chewing, slowly, very slowly. Her tongue made a lump in her cheek like a burrowing animal as she felt around her mouth. Then her face puckered up and she spit out the gift. "Yuck!"

"Charlotte ate ants!" Leo crowed. Johnny doubled over, laughing so hard he cried.

Charlotte cried, too, in fury. Her friends clustered around cooing and sending angry looks at Johnny and Leo. "I'm telling," Charlotte snarled, her nose even higher than usual.

"I didn't do anything," Leo protested, while Johnny moaned with laughter. "I didn't do it," Leo repeated.

Ivy spoke up. "Telling what? That you were so greedy you finished your own and wanted more? That you stuffed food in your mouth without even looking at it?"

"Oh, mind your own business," Charlotte snapped. But she headed toward the water fountain instead of the bench where Miss Wiltshire sat.

Ivy helped Johnny stand up. She patted him on the back. He took gulps of air. But the laughs wouldn't stop.

The bell for assembly rang, and Miss Wiltshire hurried the class inside. "Quickly, quickly, children. Mustn't be late on the very last day." She led them down the hall, into the crowded auditorium and nodded to their row with her finger pressed to her lips. Charlotte never had a chance to tattle.

The principal greeted them with a big smile, rocking back and forth on his toes, his hands folded on his round stomach like a roly-poly doll. His face was pink and his collar and tie looked tight and hot.

"I bet he's glad it's the last day," Leo whispered.

"Not as glad as I am," Johnny said. He palmed Leo a stick of gum.

The end-of-the-year speech was always the same: be careful, wear your bike helmet, don't swim at the quarry, read lots of books, obey your parents, don't litter, come back smarter than you are now.

Then each classroom teacher handed out report cards. When Miss Wiltshire gave Leo his, she winked again. What does she mean? Leo wondered. Back at his seat, Leo held his breath as he slid the card out of the envelope. On the front was his name and grade: Leo Nolan, 3W. Inside were all his grades: S for satisfactory, NI for needs improvement, a few C's for commendable. But no mention of promotion. Leo's stomach tightened. Then he noticed the girl beside him looking on the back of her report card. He turned his over. "Promoted to Grade 4," he read. "Yes!" he said, with relief.

The countdown had begun. "Nine. Eight. Seven." The voices rose to a shriek. *"Six. Five. Four. Three. Two. One!"* The auditorium echoed with cheers and screams. Kids stamped their feet and hollered.

"Good-bye, good-bye," the teachers said to their backs as children poured out the doors, emptying the room in a few seconds. "Have a wonderful summer," Miss Wiltshire called.

"We will!" Leo and Johnny promised.

Stealing Bases

Leo and Johnny had the raft at the lake all to themselves. At first, it was crowded with sunbathing high school girls, but Leo and Johnny swamped it with cannonball splashes. The girls yelled, "Monsters," "Brats," "Little stinkers." But they cleared off and paddled back to shore, leaving a rainbow slick of suntan oil to mark their trail.

"They swim like dogs with their heads out," Johnny said.

"Like seals," Leo said.

"Seals look like dogs wearing bathing caps," Johnny said. "I saw some up close in Maine."

Satisfied that the girls weren't coming back for revenge, the boys sprawled belly up on the boards. A motorboat wake gently rocked the raft. Nearby, a fish jumped up and plopped back under the water. From the beach came sounds of children's laughter, mothers calling, and the lifeguard's whistle.

"You trying out for summer baseball this afternoon?" Johnny asked. "I hope I get a base this time."

"A lot of guys will be away at camp or on vacation. We'll get bases," Leo said.

Johnny made a popping sound with his finger in the corner of his mouth. "It's a hit. Ringer's made it to first. He's running, running. He slides. Safe!"

That afternoon Leo fished under his bed for his cleats. His glove was on his closet shelf. His cap still had a good curve to the brim. Dusting it off with a shake, he pulled it on firmly, glared in the mirror, and tried to look tough.

"If you're ready, Leo," his mother called, "I'll drive you to the field on my way to the library." Leo filled a water bottle and let the screen door bang behind him as he ran toward the car. His mother dropped him off near the bleachers and he jogged toward third base. But someone was already standing on it. Someone with a baseball cap pulled down low. Leo couldn't tell who it was at first but as he got closer, he recognized Ivy.

"I'm playing third," Leo said.

"I got here first," Ivy said. "Anyway, the coaches decide who plays what base."

"I want third."

"I've got it," Ivy said. She stomped on the base to prove it.

"Why are you here anyway?" Leo said. "This tryout is for boys."

"Says who? Lots of girls are here."

"You're nuts," Leo said.

"Look around." Ivy waved her arm, and Leo saw at least a dozen other girls on the field, ready to play.

"Okay, everybody," the director said, "heads up!" Leo had no choice except to move into the outfield. "If you get the ball, try to throw it home. If you can't throw that far, aim for a player you can reach. Keep the ball coming back in fast. Understand?"

Leo put his hand up to shield his eyes from the long rays of the sun setting behind the catcher's cage. Two players grabbed air as the ball careened out of reach. Probably girls, Leo thought with a sneer. Girls can't catch.

The next ball traveled low to the ground straight at Leo. He dove with outstretched arms on the dusty grass and missed.

"Come on in now. Let's see you bat," the league director shouted.

Several players got a hit on their first swing. Only two missed all three pitches. They sat a little apart from the others on the bleachers, heads down. Leo figured they wished they hadn't bothered to show up today.

When it was Johnny's turn, Ivy called, "Go for it, Ringer! Smash that ball!" Johnny grinned and gave a thumbs-up. He doesn't care if the girls ruin the tryouts, Leo thought, shaking his head in disbelief. Johnny got a hit. The coach wrote a note on his clipboard. Now it was Leo's turn.

"Blast that ball, Leo," Ivy called. Leo ignored her. He tried to remember everything his coach had told him in the spring. Look at the ball. Step into the pitch. He tried to do all those things, but the first pitch slipped right past him. He missed the second pitch, too.

"You're swinging high," the catcher said. "Bend your knees."

Leo tried, but he was nervous and excited. Don't miss. Please don't miss, he said to himself. He didn't want to be one of the guys in the bleachers hanging his head like a sad dog.

"Ready?" the pitcher called. Leo nodded. He swung and the ball glanced off the side of the bat.

"Next batter," the coach said.

Leo took a seat beside Johnny. When Ivy was up at bat, Johnny cheered for her. "Knock it out of the park, Ivy," he called.

Leo jabbed Johnny hard in the side. "Don't root for her," he said.

"Ouch! Why not?"

"The girls will wreck the whole league."

"Why? They'd play softball but there're no summer teams. That's why they're here, Ivy told me. They're better than a lot of guys," Johnny said.

That was exactly why Leo was worried.

"Getting dark. Mosquitoes are hungry," the coach said. "You'll hear what team you're on in a few days. Thanks for coming out."

That night, Leo dreamed he was the only boy on an all-girls team. Balls flew by him, his teammates throwing hard, much stronger than he was. And they ran fast, too, while he moved like a peanut in caramel. Balls came at him and he missed them. Runners slid toward the base and he couldn't tag them. This was a nightmare!

The next morning after breakfast, Leo was surprised when Ivy rang his doorbell. She carried her bat and glove. "Want to practice?" she asked. "I'm meeting Johnny at the park. We're going to play stealing bases."

"No, thanks," Leo said. "I got plans." Stealing bases, he thought with a grunt, that's the perfect game for you.

Leo watched Ivy walk down his front path. She picked her bicycle up off the sidewalk and rode away. All morning, Leo practiced throwing and catching off the side of his house. The ball made a satisfying *thwap!* every time it hit the wall. Finally Mrs. Nolan called out the window, "Leo, please, I'm starting to twitch. Find someone to play with. Where's Johnny?"

"Playing catch with Ivy."

"So join them! Give me some quiet so I can get this work finished."

Leo knew it was an order. He rode his bicycle around the rim of the park, his glove dangling from the handlebars. No one was in sight. Ivy and Johnny must have quit already, he guessed. He practiced catching pop-ups by himself but quickly got bored.

Three days later the coach called. Three days of Johnny saying, "Did you hear?" Three nights of Leo worrying before he went to sleep, hoping that he wouldn't have another baseball nightmare. Finally, the phone rang and Eleanor called, "For you, Dogboy."

"This is Coach Truesdale. You're on the Giants. Practice tomorrow at five. Wear cleats and bring your glove and plenty of water."

Leo hung up the phone. Everyone made one team or another. But would he get a base? He might not know until after practice. Maybe not until the first game.

Leo rode to practice, left his bike by the fence, and walked down the slope towards the field. The first person he saw was Ivy.

"Hi, Leo," she said. "You're on the Giants, too?"

The second person he saw was Rose-Ellen McCoy. The third was a girl he recognized from camp. The fourth was practicing her pitching with the coach.

"Okay, sweetie. Let her rip. Right over the plate. That's the way. Good girl!" the coach bellowed. From the way the coach called her sweetie, Leo guessed that the pitcher was his daughter. A girl for a pitcher and she was the coach's daughter. This was so embarrassing. He spotted a few boys in the outfield throwing grounders and pop-ups to each other and headed out to join them.

"Some team," he said to the nearest boy. "I can't believe we have so many girls."

"I hope I get a base," the boy said. "I'm not so sure now."

"They should have their own league," Leo said. "They'll slow the whole game down." He threw to a boy who was farther away but the ball fell short. The other guy had to run in and scoop it up off the grass. "Sorry," Leo said.

The coach called the team. When they were all seated, Leo counted twelve players: five girls and eight boys—not quite as bad as his dream. Ivy caught his eye and smiled. He pretended he didn't see. When the coach gave out uniforms, Leo got number five. Pitcher, catcher, first, second, third. Maybe it means I'll play third base, Leo thought.

". . . try different positions this summer," the coach was saying. "We're a team. Remember that. Teams win, not players. Play hard, come to practice, cheer for each other, and we'll have a great time."

For the rest of the practice Leo tried to shine. He slid into first base even when the throw had arrived way ahead of him. He tried to throw the ball home from the outfield, but it landed beside second base. He swung his bat so hard his body twisted like a stick of licorice. "Easy, easy," the coach said. "Get the stroke first, then add the power."

Ivy bicycled home beside Leo. She either hadn't noticed his grumpiness or she was ignoring it. The evening light slanted low between the trees. The breeze smelled of mown grass. It carried a light spray from sprinklers, cooling Leo's face. Tangy barbecue smoke reminded him that it was dinnertime.

"I better get a base." Leo didn't realize he had spoken out loud, so he was surprised when Ivy answered.

"Didn't you hear the coach? He isn't giving permanent positions," Ivy said.

"No positions?"

"You didn't hear him?"

"I must have been daydreaming," Leo said.

"We're going to rotate. Everybody gets to try everything. Here's my street. See you," Ivy said.

Leo cycled on by himself, going slow. No positions? "That stinks!" he said aloud. A little girl playing hopscotch by herself looked up in surprise.

Leo's father stood by the barbecue wearing his chef's hat and a striped apron. Leo slumped on the porch swing. "We're going to rotate positions this year. Stupid, huh?" Leo shook his head in disgust.

"You'll get a lot of experience." Mr. Nolan slid the hamburgers onto a platter. *"Dinner!"* he hollered.

Eleanor kicked open the kitchen door and carried a bowl of steaming corn to the picnic table. Mrs. Nolan followed with the salad bowl. Leo grabbed an ear of corn as soon as he sat down. Eleanor pretended to jab his hand with her fork. "Wait until everyone's seated, Dogboy," she said.

"As if you ever waited," Leo said.

"Enough," Mrs. Nolan warned. "Pass the corn, Leo, please. Who's on your team?"

Leo gulped his lemonade. "Ivy," he said.

"There are girls on the team? That's nice," Mrs. Nolan said.

"It's terrible! There's no softball in the summer so the girls tried out for baseball. They'll get all the best positions."

"I thought you said there were no positions," Mr. Nolan said.

"The girls will get played the most. I can tell."

"Girls are just naturally more talented," said Eleanor. "Face it, Dogboy."

"Don't tease your brother, Eleanor," Mrs. Nolan said.

"Who's teasing? I'm educating him."

Leo's teeth were stuck in an ear of corn. He could never think of an answer fast enough to get the last word with Eleanor.

At the next practice, Leo stood in the outfield with nothing to do while a parade of people played the bases, too many for Leo to keep track. He tried not to sulk, but it seemed as if he was the only player the coach didn't try at a base.

"Why won't he give me a chance?" Leo complained to Johnny the next day as they were throwing high flies and grounders in Leo's backyard. "He hates me."

"I wish our coach would switch positions more," Johnny said. "I hate shortstop. When I miss a grounder, I feel like dirt. I eat dirt, too. Everybody kicks it up running to first base."

"At least you're in the action. In the outfield, the only thing that happens is little bugs get in my nose," Leo said.

That evening after dinner, Leo helped his father water the garden. "Dad, could you call the coach? Tell him to give me a base."

"You'll get to play a base, Leo, just not all the time."

"I hate playing with girls."

"Why?" asked Mr. Nolan.

"They aren't any good," Leo said.

His father raised his eyebrows. "Maybe they're too good," he guessed.

After his father had turned off the sprinkler, coiled the hose, and gone inside to watch TV, Leo sat on the porch swing watching the fireflies flash along the hedge. If there were no girls on the team, the coach would have given out positions. Rotating positions was just an excuse so the girls wouldn't look so bad. We'll lose every game, every single game in the whole season, Leo thought with a groan. If I had just one wish I'd make them disappear. One wave of the magic wand and—zap—no girls.

The magic wand made Leo think of potions, spells, and curses. I could make a voodoo doll and stick pins in it, he thought. I could use one of Eleanor's old Barbies. This idea cheered him up. He knew it wouldn't work but it would be fun. How hard was Barbie anyway? he wondered. Maybe he'd have to use a hammer and nails!

Leo found Eleanor in the kitchen making fudge, with the radio blaring. "Don't even think of asking if you can lick the bowl, Dogboy," she yelled over the music. "Every drop is mine."

"Do you have any dolls you don't want anymore?" Leo asked.

"Do I look like I have dolls?"

Leo shrugged. "Maybe you keep some around for practicing tattoos?"

"Not a bad idea," Eleanor admitted. "They might be in a box in the basement. You know Mom's thing about saving our childhood memories. So corny!" Just then the fudge began to boil. Eleanor had to stir it, so she didn't have time to ask him why he wanted a doll. Leo slipped away fast. She'd tease him forever if he told her his plan.

Mrs. Nolan saved all their old books and toys. She packed them in boxes labeled with their names and stacked these in a dry corner of the basement. Every so often Leo would think of a toy he had loved and retrieve it, an old fire truck that sprayed real water, or the sock monkey he used to sleep with. He brought these back upstairs for a while, but then he forgot about them again and they landed back in the basement boxes.

He found the dolls in the second box he opened, three grown-up Barbies and one little girl. This must be Barbie's kid sister, Leo thought. She was wearing jeans and sneakers, and her feet weren't bent into question marks like the big Barbies. She was perfect. Baseball Bonnie, Leo named her. He stacked the boxes again and carried Baseball Bonnie up to his room.

Baseball Bonnie needed a baseball cap and a glove.

Leo had no experience making doll clothes. He couldn't ask his mother for help, not without giving away his scheme or having to answer a zillion questions. Maybe there's stuff in the sewing box I can use, he thought.

The sewing box was on a shelf in the linen closet. His mother only used it when she had to sew buttons or hems that came unraveled. Leo carried it quickly back to his room. Inside, he found squares of black and brown fabric, iron-on patches for the knees of his pants. He folded a scrap of black fabric and pinned it on Baseball Bonnie's head. If he squinted, it looked almost like a baseball cap worn backward. For the glove, he cut a flat shape out of brown fabric and glued it to the doll's hand.

"Almost ready," he said. Too bad he didn't have a

candle, but it wasn't worth the risk. His parents were strict about playing with fire. They even made him blow out birthday candles fast. So he turned off the lights for atmosphere. The moon was rising behind the pine trees in the yard next door and it filled the room with a spooky glow.

Leo rummaged in the sewing box for a large needle, pricking his finger twice before he found one. He reminded himself that voodoo wasn't real and Bonnie was only a piece of plastic. He held the doll's arm between his fingers. The plastic was hard and smooth. He aimed the needle at the little arm and took a deep breath. Then he stopped. Even though he didn't believe in voodoo or Ouija boards or even wishbones, the back of his neck prickled and he shivered. With a shake of his head, Leo put the doll down and turned the lights back on. From the den he heard laughter. He wanted to be there with the rest of the family. He stuffed the doll into the bottom drawer of his bureau, put the sewing box away, and went downstairs to join the others in front of the television. For a while he forgot all about Baseball Bonnie.

In the first game of the summer, Leo's team played the Dodgers. The coach gave out positions after the warm-up. "Nolan, take third base," he said.

Leo jabbed his fist in the air and muttered, *"Yes!"* under his breath. The coach told Ivy to play left field.

She waved at Leo as she passed him. She didn't seem to mind playing outfield.

Leo shook out his arms and swung them like windmills to loosen up. The first two pitches were high, and the third was a strike.

"Doing fine," the coach called to the pitcher. "Doing great. Take your time, sweetie." Leo winced. Does he have to call her "sweetie" in front of the other team? he wondered.

On the next pitch, the batter sent the ball flying toward third base. Leo lunged, but it hit a tuft of grass and veered out of reach, skipping and bouncing into the outfield. Lying on his belly, Leo saw Ivy scoop up the ball and fire it to second, stopping the batter at first base.

"Good play," the coach called to Ivy.

The next inning, Ivy played second base and Leo was in center field. "Back me up, Leo," Ivy said.

She can't mean that, Leo thought, as he stood in the outfield shielding his eyes with his glove. She'd never miss a ball like I did.

The inning crept by. The only action in center field was three crows arguing over a stolen hamburger bun. Finally his team went in.

Just before Leo went to bat, Ivy whispered, "Imagine the ball moving in slow motion and swing smooth." The girl ahead of Leo struck out. With Ivy's words in mind, Leo stepped to the plate. Please, please let me get on base, he thought, starting to tense up. He tried to follow Ivy's advice. He bent his knees and tried to relax.

The first pitch was high and Leo didn't swing. "Ball," the umpire called.

The next pitch came in straight. Swing smooth, Leo told himself. He pretended the ball was slowing down and he swung the bat in an even arc. *Pow!* The ball sailed out, too high for the infielders, too low for the outfielders. A double. A runner crossed home plate. With Leo on second and a man on third, the Giants could score again this inning. Leo waved to Ivy. Her advice had worked.

It was Ivy's turn at bat. Come on, Ivy, Leo thought. A double, please.

Ivy stepped up to the plate. The first two pitches were low and she didn't swing. The third pitch went outside. If the pitcher missed one more, Ivy walked and the bases would be loaded. The pitcher took off his cap and scratched his head.

Ivy held the bat a few inches off her shoulder. The pitcher wound up and threw the ball fast and wild. Before Ivy could jump aside, it smashed her, hard. She dropped the bat and gasped, rubbing her arm and hopping up and down.

"Take your base," the umpire told Ivy. "Control that

ball or you're out of the game," he warned the pitcher.

Ivy walked to first base. Leo saw her wipe her eyes with the back of her hand.

Bases were loaded now, Ivy on first, Leo on second, and Bill on third. Ann Marie stepped up to bat. The pitcher fired his first pitch fast and inside, forcing her to jump back.

He's doing it on purpose, Leo realized. He's trying to hit her, too.

"Get that ball under control or I'll throw you out," the umpire yelled, his face red. "Last warning."

The next pitch came over the plate. Ann Marie slammed it, sending all three runners home before getting tagged at third. The Giants were ahead by four.

Leo and Ivy sat out the next inning. Walking past the Dodger's pitcher, Leo heard him mutter, ". . . a girl get a hit off me? . . . make 'em cry . . . shouldn't be here." The catcher had a hand on the pitcher's arm to calm him.

Leo sat down on the bench beside Ivy. "He nailed you on purpose," Leo said, telling her what he'd overheard.

She shook her head in disgust. "He tried to hit Ann Marie, too. He thinks he can scare us into quitting."

The Dodgers scored four runs to tie the game. "How's your arm?" the coach asked Ivy.

"Okay," she said with a wobbly smile.

"Sure you want to play in the last inning?" the coach asked. Ivy nodded her head fiercely. "Take second base," he said. "Leo, try shortstop and keep an eye out for Ivy in case she needs any help."

Leo glanced over at Ivy who was rubbing her arm. Her arm! Suddenly he remembered Baseball Bonnie and the voodoo needle! Leo felt himself blush. How could I ever do that? Ivy's better than I am, he admitted to himself. I'm lucky she's on my team. Good thing I didn't push the needle in.

The score was still tied, four runs each, with the Giants up last. The Dodger pitcher strutted to the mound pounding his fist into his glove. He pulled his cap down low and kicked his leg up like a kung-fu fighter. With six fast strikes, he finished off the first two batters. Then Ivy stepped up to the plate. The pitcher glared and twisted his toe in the dirt as if he was squishing a beetle.

Come on, Ivy, Leo thought. Don't let him scare you. You've got as much right as anybody to be in this game.

The first pitch came fast. Ivy flinched. "Strike one," the umpire called.

"You can do it, Ivy," Leo called. "Send that ball on a *long* ride."

She stepped back from the next pitch, too.

Leo leaped to his feet. "Show him, Ivy!" he shout-

ed. "Blast it right at him. You can win this game!"

Ivy pivoted and grinned at Leo, then raised her bat for the pitch. This time she stood firm and swung hard, connecting with a *crack!* The ball flew high over second base, out into center field. Farther, farther, farther, *farther! Home Run!*

The Giants jumped and clapped while Ivy ran the bases. The Dodger pitcher spit in the dirt, disgusted. Ivy rounded third and came down the base line slapping her teammates' hands. She stomped on home plate with two feet, then turned to Leo and gave him high fives with both hands. "I heard you," she said. "I was scared of getting nailed again. Then I heard your voice and I knew I could do it. You said so."

Ivy's run won the game. After all the cheers and slaps on the back, Ivy rode her bike home with Leo as the evening faded into shadows, victory grins on both their faces.

"Want to play stealing bases tomorrow?" Leo asked.

Ivy nodded and waved good-bye as she turned onto her street. Leo cycled on by himself. He laughed out loud as he remembered Ivy's hit and the expression on the pitcher's face. Three little girls were jumping rope on the sidewalk. "Go get 'em, girls," Leo called as he rode by.

It's a Deal, Dogboy

"**N**o, you may *not* buy firecrackers. They're *dangerous*. You can lose an eye or a hand, or blow out your eardrums."

Mrs. Nolan gave this speech every year. Even sparklers made her nervous. Leo kept hoping that maybe this year he'd think of something to say to change her mind. But she shook her head and went right on pulling weeds from between the tomato plants. "We have to stake these tomatoes," she said to Leo's father. "Look at them! They're sprawling everywhere."

Leo tried his father. "You had firecrackers when you were a kid, Dad. If you did it, why can't I?"

"Your mother's right. Firecrackers are dangerous."

"Come on, Dad. You know they're fun. I'm tired of

snakes and sparklers. Those are for babies." Leo turned over a rock with the toe of his sneaker and watched a fat pink worm burrow back underground. "All I need is five dollars. I won't ask for anything else all summer. I promise."

Mr. Nolan slapped a mosquito on his neck. "How about this year we don't stake the tomatoes? Let them alone and see how they do. Experiment."

Mrs. Nolan sat back on her heels and snorted. "The worms will have a feast. I am not experimenting on the tomatoes, thank you. I plan to eat tomatoes all summer, ripe and juicy, sliced fresh with chopped basil. I want lots and lots of tomatoes, enough to make spaghetti sauce. You don't want to drive down to the hardware store and buy stakes. You'd rather lie in that hammock and read your mystery."

"What about my firecrackers?" Leo insisted.

"Don't whine, Leo. We already said *no* firecrackers," his mother said in her "that's final" voice.

Leo left his parents discussing tomatoes and went inside. Eleanor was sitting at the kitchen table painting her toenails black. She had dyed her hair black this summer, and she outlined her eyes in black every morning before she came down to breakfast. Most of her clothes were black, too.

"Looks like you stubbed your foot on a boulder or got stepped on by an elephant," Leo told her.

"Thanks. You look good, too, Dogboy. How about letting me pierce your ear? I need to practice. I'm going into business."

"How much will you charge?"

"Five bucks for an ear, ten for a nose or belly button, fifteen for an eyebrow."

Leo cringed at the thought.

"But I'll do you for free for the practice," Eleanor said. "I'll even lend you an earring to wear while your ear heals. It won't hurt. I'll freeze your ear with an ice cube. Don't you want to look cool?" She started on her fingernails, carefully layering on the shiny polish stroke by stroke.

Leo watched Eleanor finish one hand and hold her stubby, now-black nails out to admire. He needed the money. "I'll let you do it if you pay me ten bucks," Leo said.

"Pay you? I do you a favor and *I* pay *you?* Why would I do that?"

"Because I'm the guinea pig," Leo said. He thought of Patches, his pet guinea pig. He would never let Eleanor do anything cruel to Patches. "It might hurt. You're just getting started. You know how some doctors are good at giving shots and others hurt like anything? You need practice. I bet it will hurt a lot."

Leo could tell he had made a good point. But he'd also scared himself. It might hurt as much as getting

Novocain. Eleanor might be worse than the nurse who tried to test his blood last year and couldn't find a vein. "I don't think I want to."

Eleanor had finished both hands and was waving them in the air to make the nail polish dry faster. She looked like a lady vampire with her outlined eyes and dull black hair. Last summer Eleanor's hair had been short and brown. She played croquet with him and did jigsaws with their mother on the porch table. She'd even built a tree house behind the garage. Leo remembered her long legs dangling over the side as she hauled up a bucket filled with lemonade, cookies, and grapes. She sure had changed. Leo missed the old Eleanor. This summer it would be a waste of time to ask her to play croquet. He knew she'd say no.

"Three bucks," she said.

"Five and your tree house," Leo bargained.

"That old thing? Okay, it's a deal, Dogboy. Come up to my room."

"Now? I can't do it now," Leo said.

"It will only take a few minutes," Eleanor said.

"I'm busy now," Leo stalled.

"You don't look busy."

"I've got to go over to Johnny's. How about tonight after supper?"

Eleanor nodded, narrowing her dark eyes. She looked witchy with her dark hair and white face.

"Don't back out, Dogboy. You made a deal."

Leo rode his bike to Johnny's. He tried not to think about the needle going through his earlobe. It will just be a prick, he thought. A hard pinch. It couldn't hurt much. Once he'd sewn his fingers together with thread, pushing the needle through the skin at the tips. He'd pretended he was a puppeteer, drawing his fingers in and out by pulling the thread. It hadn't hurt. But his ear was softer than his fingertips. At least he hadn't agreed to let Eleanor pierce his nose or eyebrow.

Johnny was watering the front garden. He waved the hose toward Leo as he rode up.

"Go ahead," Leo said. "It'll cool me off."

Johnny aimed the spray of water at Leo's head, then turned the hose back toward the garden. "I'm working. My grandfather's paying me to weed. I'm going to buy some firecrackers."

"What kind?"

"Roman candles and bottle rockets if I have enough money. If I just have a little, then I'll buy cherry bombs and strings of little firecrackers. How about you? Got any money?"

"Not yet. Eleanor's going to pay me five bucks if I let her pierce my ear."

"Five bucks? How's she going to do it?" Johnny asked.

"With a needle," Leo said.

"She's going to poke a needle through your ear?"

Leo nodded.

"For five bucks?"

Leo nodded again. "She freezes the ear with an ice cube."

"Do you think she'd pay me, too?" Johnny asked. "It sounds easier than pulling weeds."

"Ask her," Leo said. "And you know what else? She's giving me the tree house, too. We'll have a place to go all summer. We can put our comics there and food. We can even sleep out."

Johnny finished watering and coiled the hose. "Let's go see it," he said.

They left their bikes by Leo's garage. The tree house was out back with three slats of wood nailed to the trunk for footholds. Leo climbed up first. "You need both hands to climb," he told Johnny. Soon they both sat crosslegged surrounded by thick rustling leaves.

"It's like a big green room," Johnny said, "like we're in a forest somewhere with nobody around."

Leo lay on his back, looked up, and glimpsed a few bits of sky between the green. "I wonder what it's like when it rains. We probably wouldn't even get wet."

"Let's sleep here tonight," Johnny said. "My grandfather has old army stuff he'll lend us."

Leo agreed. "My parents' old sleeping bags are in the basement and I've got a flashlight, too." Then he remembered Eleanor and he winced as if jabbed by a toothache. "But tonight I get my ear pierced."

"That won't take long, will it?" Johnny said.

"It better not," Leo said.

"I'm going to watch first," Johnny said.

Leo wished he could be the one who watched. Still, five dollars would buy a bunch of firecrackers. I should have let her do it right away, Leo thought. He rubbed his ears. "Which side should I let her pierce?"

Johnny tilted his head to the side, squinting. "Turn left," he said. "Now right." Then he shrugged. "I don't know. They look alike."

"Of course they look alike. They're my ears."

"So? I bet some people's ears don't match. Do your hands match?" Johnny asked.

Leo stared at his hands and then placed them palm to palm. "Of course they match. Why wouldn't they?"

"Why should they?" Johnny said. "Some people's eyes don't match. They have one brown and one green, or one blue and one brown."

"Is that true?" Leo said.

Johnny nodded. "I read it in a magazine at the barber's. There was another story, too, about a hamster that got loose in a car and ate the insides. It wrecked the whole thing, one little hamster. And there was a picture of a baby that turned out to be an alien. It was some magazine. I would have bought it if it was for sale."

"That's even weirder than Eleanor," Leo said, standing up. "Let's get this place ready for tonight."

All afternoon the boys collected things. Johnny's grandfather gave them a box of his army equipment: canteen, blankets, mess kit, and even a canvas tent.

"We can hang the tent up in the corner," Johnny suggested, "in case of rain."

Mrs. Nolan showed them the old camping supplies piled in the basement, covered by a layer of dust. Leo and Johnny carried the sleeping bags up to the tree house, plus three brown cushions from the old playroom couch, two milk crates, and a square metal box with a clasp for a lock. "For valuables," Leo said. He wasn't sure what valuables they would ever have. The box made him think of pirates and buried treasure.

"We can keep food in it so the raccoons won't steal it," Johnny said.

The tent and the sleeping bags smelled musty, and the blankets had the sharp odor of mothballs. The boys draped them over the edge of the platform.

"I got to go. My grandfather's making ravioli for dinner," Johnny said. "I don't want to be late. See you later. Don't let Eleanor do anything until I come over."

That evening, Leo would have been happy to have

an excuse to stall the ear business, but Johnny rang the doorbell before the Nolans had even started dessert. Mrs. Nolan told Leo to get another dish and spoon for Johnny. She served ice cream to everyone and passed around a bowl of sliced strawberries. Leo tried to eat slowly, scraping little curls of ice cream onto his spoon. He still had a big scoop left when everyone else had finished. "That's a first." Mr. Nolan laughed. "You feeling sick, Leo?"

"What's the matter, Dogboy? Feeling like you might have the *chicken* pox?" Eleanor teased.

"Please don't call your brother that terrible name. It's insulting and mean," Mrs. Nolan said.

"It's just a joke, Mom. Leo doesn't mind, do you, Leo?"

Leo shrugged and kept on eating tiny spoonfuls of ice cream.

"At least she doesn't call you Dogbreath," Johnny pointed out.

Mr. Nolan massaged the back of his neck. "You're right, of course, Johnny. It could be worse."

Eleanor asked to be excused. "I'll see you upstairs," she said to Leo. "Come on up as soon as you're finished." She made chicken noises as she left the room: "Cluck, cluck-cluck, clu-uck."

Leo tried to make his ice cream last as long as he could. Finally, he and Johnny sat at the table alone,

Johnny with an empty bowl, Leo staring at a puddle of melted ice cream. "It'll be dark if we wait much longer," Johnny said.

They carried their bowls into the kitchen. Upstairs, Eleanor's door was closed. Leo knocked. "It's me," he said.

"Come on in and shut the door," Eleanor said. She was lying on her bed, smoking a cigarette.

"I didn't know you smoked," Leo said.

"I do now."

"That's dumb," Johnny said. "My grandfather messed up his lungs smoking. He said he wishes he'd never started."

Eleanor blinked slowly in mock boredom. "Watch this," she said. She crossed her legs, put the cigarette between her toes and leaned forward to take a puff. "Cool, huh? No hands. And this. Watch." When she made her lips into an O she looked just like a big-eyed cartoon fish. Out came smoke in the shape of small rings that stretched into wider circles as they floated upward.

Eleanor took the cigarette from her toes and snuffed it out in the saucer that served as her ashtray. "Ready?" she asked Leo.

He didn't bother to answer. Five dollars, he reminded himself. "Give me the money first," he said.

"Don't you trust me?"

"If I hold the money, it will keep me from thinking about the needle," he said.

Eleanor counted out five crumpled one-dollar bills from the bottom of her Doc Martins.

"That's where you keep your money?" Johnny said.

"It's safe there. Who'd put their hand inside my smelly shoe?" she asked.

Leo smoothed out the bills, folded them over, and put them in his pocket. "Where's the needle?" he said.

Eleanor held it up. "I have to sterilize it." She lit a match and put the tip of the needle in the center of the flame until it glowed red. Blowing out the match with one quick puff, she waved the needle in the air. "To cool it down," she explained. "But I forgot the ice. Dogboy, run downstairs and grab some ice, okay? Tell the ancients it's for drinks."

"They're not ancient," Leo said, feeling oddly protective of his parents who were probably sitting on the porch peacefully sipping coffee in the twilight. He wished he was down there with them, lying on the porch swing, listening to the drone of grown-up conversation. That was the safe haven, and this was the den of danger. "They're not even fifty yet."

"Ancient is a state of mind, not a birth date, Dogboy. Just get the ice."

Leo was back in a few minutes carrying a blue plastic ice cube tray. "Want an ice cube to chew on?" he offered Johnny.

Eleanor took the tray from him and made him sit on her desk chair. "Don't move," she warned. "Once I start, it's important to stay perfectly still. You're Mount Rushmore, okay? You are made of stone. Except for your ear."

"I want to see the needle," Leo said.

"Don't touch the point," she said, handing it to him carefully.

"Why is the tip all black?" Leo asked.

"It looks dirty," Johnny said.

"That's from the match. First it turns red and then black."

"Why?" Leo said.

"Who knows, who cares, Dogboy. You're stalling. Here, hold this ice against your ear." Eleanor sandwiched Leo's earlobe between two ice cubes.

"It tickles," Leo complained.

"How far in will the needle go?" Johnny asked.

"All the way through."

Leo shivered. Now it was real, a real needle pushing through his very real ear. Pushing all the way through, from one side to the other. "What's the ear made of?" he asked.

"It's an ear, stupid," Eleanor said with a groan. "You

two are such losers. What is this anyway, medical school? Ask Mr. Science? Your ear is your ear, that's all."

"Is it bone? Is it muscle?" Leo persisted.

"It's ear, dummy. Skin and ear," Eleanor said.

"Have you ever done this before?" Johnny asked.

Eleanor picked up the needle and reached for Leo's ear.

Leo leaned away from her. "Am I your first time?"

"There's got to be a first," Eleanor said. She reached again.

"Wait, wait, wait, wait, wait," Leo said. He stood up. His hand was numb from holding the ice cubes, and his shoulder was wet from the drips. "You might mess up. I could get infected. The needle might break off in my ear. It will hurt, I can tell."

"Good grief!" Eleanor groaned. "You are such a geek, Leo. I can't believe you're backing out. I'm all set here. Everything's ready. It would just take a minute and that's all. One little minute. You made a deal, Dogboy. I paid you already."

"So here's the money," Leo said. He pulled it out of his pocket and dropped it on Eleanor's dresser, on top of the clutter of bottles, cotton balls, and crumpled tissues. "Come on, Johnny. Let's get more food for the tree house."

Leo and Johnny had reached the top of the stairs

when Eleanor called, "Hey Dogboy, you can't spend the night in my tree house."

"You gave it to me," Leo protested.

"Un-uh," Eleanor said. "It was part of the deal you just backed out of. No ear, no tree house."

"Oh come on, Eleanor. You don't want it anymore," Leo said.

"So what? I built it. It's mine."

Leo's face flushed. He and Johnny had spent the whole day setting up the tree house, dragging supplies, begging for equipment, picking out candy and comics. Now she said it wasn't his! If he had been younger he would have run back into her room and grabbed her stringy dyed hair and pulled a clump right out of her head, he was so mad. Once he'd broken every crayon in her brand new sixty-four-color box, snapped every one of them in half with a satisfying crack because she'd made him mad. But he was smarter now. He really wanted the tree house.

He walked back into her room. She was lying on her bed with her hands folded under her head, looking as smug as Sylvester when he thinks he's got Tweety Bird trapped under a teacup.

"I'll pay you for it," Leo said.

Eleanor swung her foot in circles. "How much?"

"Five bucks," Leo said.

"Fifteen," she countered.

"That's crazy," Leo said. "It's just a bunch of boards."

"Fifteen," she repeated.

"It will take me weeks to get that much."

"I can wait," she said.

Johnny tapped Leo on the shoulder and motioned for him to come out in the hall. They sat on the top step of the stairs, shoulder to shoulder. "I've got three bucks," Johnny said. "I was saving it for firecrackers."

"I've got two," Leo admitted.

"So that's five," Johnny said. "We can earn the rest weeding for my grandfather. I bet your parents will pay us for work, too. We should buy it from her."

"It's not worth it," Leo said. "She's a robber and a jerk."

"It'll be great," Johnny said. "We can practically live up there. Say yes. It's better than letting her shove that needle into your ear." He squeezed his own earlobe. "An ear is more than just skin."

Leo sighed. "I wish I'd been born first in this family. Or I could have been an only child. Or we could have been brothers. Instead I've got the weird witch for a sister and she's robbing me. Me, her baby brother. But what can we do?"

With their arms around each other's shoulders, Leo and Johnny walked back to Eleanor's room. "Five now and ten more by the end of the summer," Leo agreed.

"Deal," Eleanor said. "I'll write up the agreement and you can sign. Go get the money. I want it now, before you two spend the night up there. Up there with all the bats and snakes."

"There aren't any snakes," Leo said. "You can't scare us."

It was getting dark fast when they climbed the tree house ladder. Johnny's grandfather had made them candle lanterns, cans with wire handles and sand in the bottom. Johnny lit them and put the matches in the metal box. They folded the blankets and lay the sleeping bags on top of them, with the couch pillows for their heads. Then they sprayed themselves with bug spray and lay down.

The candles flickered in the cans and cast long shadows. Leo lay staring up at the thick ceiling of leaves, just visible in the candles' glow. The night was quiet.

"Another year with no firecrackers," he said.

Johnny grunted.

"My parents didn't want me to get them," Leo admitted.

"Neither did my grandfather," Johnny said.

"Now we don't have to sneak," Leo said.

"I bet my grandfather will take us to see the fireworks at the harbor," Johnny said. "They light up the whole sky. Then when they land in the water, they sizzle. It's neat."

Not as exciting as setting off our own, Leo thought. But firecrackers are over fast. Light them, boom, it's all done. The tree house would be forever. "Let's blow out the candles now, before we fall asleep," he said.

They each blew out a candle. An owl hooted faintly. The moon rose from behind a tree and turned the whole yard silver.

Magnolia

On a summer morning Leo sat by the window in the living room turning the pages in the family photo album. He stopped at the page filled with snapshots of a black-and-white dalmatian. Chief was a great dog, Leo thought. He remembered Chief's soft tongue and silky ears. At night, he'd jump on the bed and nestle up alongside Leo, resting his head on Leo's chest. In the morning, Chief's cold nose was the only alarm clock Leo needed. He remembered running with Chief in the park and playing hide-and-seek with him inside on rainy days. Chief was so smart that he could find Leo anywhere, even in the dirty clothes hamper. What a dog!

But Chief had been gone for months now, taken away by his owner, who gave Leo a reward for finding him. I won't ever find another dog as fine as Chief, Leo thought.

"Summer's the best time to get a new dog," Mrs. Nolan had said. "We'll be able to get to know it and train it. Dogs need to have time with people to form a bond. It's a good idea to wait until school's out."

Now it was, time to remind his mother about the dog. Leo found his mother in her garden, tying the roses to the trellis. "What if we go to the animal shelter and we don't find a dog we like?" he asked.

"We can check several shelters. There are at least three good shelters within an hour's drive. You'll know when you see a dog that you like."

"How will we know if the dog will get along with the cat?" Leo asked. Magoo was a large gray cat with white spots above her eye that made her look as if she were stargazing.

"Magoo can take care of herself. Dogs and cats work these things out. Don't worry so much," his mother said.

But Leo did worry. What if the dog chased Magoo up a tree? She was too lazy and too fat to ever get down. Leo would have to climb the tree and rescue her. And what if Magoo scratched the dog? She might claw him right across the nose. Then they'd never be friends. But most of all, Leo worried about finding the perfect dog. How would he know which dog to choose? He might pick a biter or a barker or a dog that chewed up his baseball cards.

I'll ask Johnny's grandfather, Leo thought. Angelo Penino always had at least two dogs living in his house, sometimes more. He found strays in the strangest places: the auto body shop, the train station, the dump, even the laundromat. He washed them and fed them. Then he taught them tricks like sit, stay, roll over. He knew more about dogs than anybody.

Leo found Mr. Penino working on his truck with his head under the hood. Two dogs lay in the shade, heads resting on their paws. When Leo walked up the driveway, the dogs looked up, ears alert. They watched him, but they didn't move. The brown one made a low growl, a warning. Mr. Penino stuck his head out to see who it was. "Be quiet, Fred, Leo's a friend."

The dogs thumped their tails. Leo scratched their heads.

"What can I do for you, Leo?"

"I came to talk to you about dogs."

"Good topic for a conversation. Can't think of many things I like more than dogs. Baseball and dogs." Mr. Penino shut the hood of his truck with a bang and wiped his hands on an oily rag hanging out of his front pocket. "I could use some lemonade. How about you?"

Leo nodded and followed him into the backyard. The dogs padded behind them and settled into a shady corner. Mr. Penino grew flowers, vegetables, grapes, even melons. An old wood table and chairs were tucked beneath the arbor. Plants sprawled and bloomed with no space wasted: tomatoes in raised beds, green tepees of climbing beans, squash and melons twining along the fence.

Mr. Penino brought out a pitcher of lemonade, two glasses, and cookies shaped like little moons on a dark blue plate.

"I'm getting a dog," Leo said.

"That's a fine idea," Mr. Penino said. He took a long drink of lemonade.

"How did you choose your dogs?" Leo asked.

"They found me, didn't you boys?" Mr. Penino said. At the sound of his voice, both dogs looked up and thumped their tails. "Have a cookie."

Leo helped himself to one of the moons. It crumbled in his mouth. "These are good."

"I make 'em for Johnny. He's like you, always hungry. Now what can I tell you about dogs?"

"How will I know which one to choose? I want a good dog. What if I pick a mean one or a dog that makes trouble?"

Mr. Penino laughed. "It's easy, Leo. You look. You pet them. You see which one you like. You see if the dog likes you. You'll know. Trust me, you will know. One dog will wag his tail a certain way, maybe bark. You'll notice and say, 'That's my dog.' "

"What if it's not a good dog? I'm afraid that I'll pick a bad dog."

Mr. Penino shook his head. "Just look carefully and pay attention to yourself. You'll know which dog is the dog for you."

Leo went home with his questions unanswered. Mr. Penino hadn't given him the kind of advice he wanted. Exactly what should he look for? How could he know which dog was the right one for him?

"Get a puppy," Eleanor said that night at dinner. "They're cute."

"Puppies take a lot of work," Mr. Nolan warned. "You have to keep an eye on them all the time. They can chew anything. They whine and yap. It's a lot of responsibility."

"They're cute," Eleanor insisted. "Get a puppy, Leo. You don't want a dog that somebody gave away, a discard. Get a puppy. You'll have more fun."

"Who's going to do all that work, training it, cleaning up its papers?" Mrs. Nolan said. "Not me, said the little red hen."

"Dogboy will do it," Eleanor said.

"Eleanor," her mother warned, "no names. Leo, do you think you want a puppy?"

"Maybe," Leo said.

"Think about it. We can visit the shelters tomorrow," his mother said. "You might get a better idea after you see some dogs."

"Neat," Eleanor said.

"Not you, Eleanor," Mrs. Nolan said. "Leo gets to choose. No outside influence."

Leo sighed in relief. It would be even harder to make the right decision with Eleanor yammering in his ear.

That night, as he was trying to sleep, Leo thought of the dogs he liked best. Chief, of course. And Uncle Ted's golden retriever, Isabel, who dove for rocks at the lake.

I want a dog who will follow me all over town and wait outside the store or on the porch when I visit a friend. A dog who sits at the window watching for me to come home from school. A dog who'll be my pillow when I lie on the rug and read. A dog who likes to play in the snow.

Leo could think of lots of dogs he didn't like: the Doberman chained in the yard near school with teeth like a killer shark's; the Chihuahua in the corner house that wore a dumb red sweater all winter. He didn't want a dog that drooled, or a dog shaped like a sausage, or a dog with strange ears or stubby legs.

The next day Mrs. Nolan and Leo drove to the Lakeside Animal Shelter. "I picked up a book about dogs at the library," Mrs. Nolan said, "just in case we need to look up a breed. Each breed has a distinct personality. It helps to know what you're in for."

"What about mutts? How can you tell with them?"

"You try and guess what sort of a mix it is and then

you hope for the best. Sort of like kids." She smiled at Leo. "Relax."

Leo cracked his knuckles absentmindedly, making his mother wince. "What if I pick the wrong dog and we hate him."

"We can always take him back to the shelter if we discover that he's really impossible. Don't worry so much. It will all work out. Trust me."

Mrs. Nolan parked under a shady tree. She took an old blanket out of the trunk and spread it on the backseat. With the dog book under her arm she walked toward the shelter.

Leo followed. He could hear dogs barking inside the building. His mother opened the door for an older woman who walked with a cane. Leo could tell she had been crying from the tear trails on her cheeks. She gave them a weak smile as she walked slowly past.

"Poor thing," Mrs. Nolan whispered to Leo as they walked into the building. "I bet she just lost a pet."

"Maybe someone will find it for her," Leo said.

"No, I meant that she had to give up her pet. Probably she couldn't take care of it anymore or she couldn't afford it."

"That's sad," Leo said. His mother nodded. Leo turned to watch the woman walk slowly toward a bus stop. She did look frail. A dog on a leash would pull her over easily if it dashed after a cat or chased a squirrel up a tree.

Inside the animal shelter, the man at the desk gave Mrs. Nolan a clipboard with an application form to fill out. "Could we look around first?" she asked. "We'd like to get an idea of what dogs are available."

"No problem," the man said. "There are a few strays and some older dogs."

"Any puppies?" Leo asked.

The man nodded his head. "Yup. The mother was a beagle and there's no telling what the father was. Probably a black Lab. Funny looking little guys. Look around. Lots of people come in here looking for a puppy and change their minds." He pointed to the kennel door.

Leo could hear the barking. When his mother opened the door, the barking grew more frantic. Rows of cages lined the aisle. "It looks like a jail," Leo whispered to his mother.

The floor of each cage was concrete. Dogs lay on their sides or stomachs. Some paced back and forth. Some pressed their noses against the wire and barked and barked. Cages at the far end held big dogs. A German shepherd circled inside his cage, whining.

"Poor thing," Mrs. Nolan said. "He's a beauty."

"He's pretty wild," the attendant said. "He might

have some wolf in him. We're not sure. Anyway, he's a stray, and we have a policy against placing strays with children. They can be vicious."

"Where are the puppies?" Leo asked.

The man pointed to a low cage in the corner. "They're still very young. Let me know if you want to take one out."

The puppies were asleep in a pile, eyes shut, plump round sides heaving with each breath. They were brown and black with a few white markings on their chests and feet. Pink noses, pointed tails, ears like velvet triangles.

"Four left, all males," the attendant said. "They'll be gone by the weekend, you can bet on it."

"How long do you keep the dogs?" Mrs. Nolan said.

"Depends on the space. We try for two weeks at least, longer if we have room."

"Then do they go to a farm or something?" Leo asked his mother.

She shook her head. "I wish that was the case. If nobody adopts them, the dogs are put to sleep."

Leo stood up and stared at her, his mouth open. "They kill them?" His voice rose in outrage.

"Sssh, Leo, it's the only thing they can do. There isn't any room to keep them. You see how crowded it is in here."

"I don't care. It's the worst thing I ever heard of.

They take these animals and they kill them."

"They try to find homes for them. They do the best job they can. It's not the shelter's fault that people don't take care of their pets."

Leo turned away from her and walked up and down the rows of cages. What would happen to all these dogs? They hadn't done anything wrong. It wasn't fair.

Leo stopped in front of a cage with a brown and white dog inside. The dog had a shiny red collar and the saddest eyes that Leo had ever seen. He put his hand up against the screen. Cautiously the dog leaned forward and sniffed his palm. Then a pink tongue licked him lightly and the dog's feathery tail tapped against the floor.

The attendant looked over. "She just arrived. Name's Magnolia. An old lady brought her in. Beautiful dog. I'd take her home myself, but my wife would turn me out of the house. We already have two."

"How old is she?" Mrs. Nolan said.

"Three or four, I think. Looks like a pedigree to me, some type of spaniel," the attendant said.

Mrs. Nolan looked up the page for spaniels and opened the dog book. Leo found a picture like the dog in the cage. Mrs. Nolan read the description. "Playful, loyal, energetic. Likes to run. Not too destructive. Good hunting dog." She smiled at Leo. "Sounds like a

good choice for you. I bet she could learn tricks. She's probably already trained. She's been well cared for. You can tell by her coat that she's been groomed and fed."

Leo was only half listening. Mostly he was watching Magnolia. And she was watching him, her head tilted to one side as if asking him a question. Well, she seemed to say, are you the one? Pick me. I'll be your dog.

"Are you sure you wouldn't rather have a puppy?" his mother asked. "This litter is a good mix for disposition if the father was a Lab. I bet they'll grow into fine dogs."

Magnolia made a sound that was part whimper and part growl, as if she were trying to talk to Leo. Her tail was wagging so much that her rear end swayed from side to side.

"Listen to her, Mom. She's talking. Isn't she pretty?"

Mrs. Nolan smiled. "Would you let this dog out so we can see her?" she asked the attendant.

"I'll bring her outside to the pen. It's fenced in so you can play with her." He pointed to a door at the end of the row of cages.

A little girl and her mother stood by the puppies' cage. "I like the one with the four white feet. I'll call him Boots," the girl said. The attendant was right, the puppies would be chosen quickly, Leo thought. But who would chose Magnolia?

The pen was surrounded by a chain-link fence. The ground was packed dirt, dusty in the hot sun. Leo waited by the gate. Soon the attendant came around the side of the building with Magnolia on a leash. She was smaller than she'd looked in the cage and she walked with a bounce, ears flopping, tail swinging as if she already knew there were good times ahead. As soon as the man unclipped her leash, she bounded toward Leo, then skidded to a stop and sat at his feet looking up at him.

"Good girl," Mrs. Nolan said. "Try throwing the ball for her. I bet she knows how to retrieve."

Leo tossed a tennis ball that was lying on the ground. The dog jumped up and ran after it, catching it as it bounced and carrying it back to Leo. She placed it at his feet, tail waving, eyes bright. Leo threw it again. "She likes to play," he said.

"She likes to play with *you*," his mother said. "She figured out what she wants. Have you made up your mind?"

Leo grinned. "You know I have, Mom."

Leo played with the dog while his mother filled out all the papers, paid the fees, and picked up Magnolia's records. She bought a leash, too, since they hadn't thought to bring one. Then Leo proudly led Magnolia to the car. "I'll sit in back with her so she isn't scared," he said. When he opened the back door, the dog jumped in with no hesitation. Leo sat beside her. He could tell she was nervous because she didn't want to sit down at first. But after a few minutes, she lay down on the seat with her head resting on his leg. She let out a big sigh and closed her eyes. All the way home Leo stroked her head. "Thanks, Mom," he said.

"You made a good choice. I never thought you'd find a dog so quickly."

"Me neither. I think she found me."

Eleanor didn't see the new dog until dinnertime, when she came home from her babysitting job. Leo didn't understand why anyone would trust Eleanor with a child. She was mean and grumpy and special-ized in small tortures like pinching the flesh on his upper arm and sticking her pointy finger hard between his ribs. Maybe she scared kids so much they didn't dare complain. But you would think the parents would notice the odd bruises on their children.

Eleanor flopped onto a kitchen chair. "I'm dying. Food, quickly please, food. I'm exhausted." Her black hair fell all over her face like the bride of Frankenstein when she first woke up after the operation.

Mrs. Nolan poured Eleanor a tall glass of orange juice. "You've got time for a shower before dinner."

Magnolia had been snoozing under the table. She

sat up on her haunches and her tail wagged against Eleanor's leg. Eleanor jumped in surprise and yelled, "A giant moth just flew by my leg."

"Look under the table," Leo said. "It's my new dog."

Eleanor's scream frightened Magnolia, who now huddled against Leo's legs.

"It's okay, Magnolia. It's just weird Eleanor," Leo comforted the dog. "Don't scream, Eleanor. It frightens her."

"You call me weird and your dog is named Magnolia? What kind of stupid name is that? Why didn't you get a puppy? I can't believe you picked this old mutt."

"She's not a mutt. She's a spaniel. She's smart and I like her. Besides she's not so old."

"Were there any puppies?" Eleanor asked.

Leo nodded. "But they weren't as nice as Magnolia. And they were all going to get chosen anyway. They didn't need homes."

"Right, chosen by smart people who know something about dogs. People who know better than to choose some old has-been reject dog."

"That's enough, Eleanor," Mrs. Nolan said. "Leo made his choice. She's a fine dog and I can tell she's happy to have a good home."

"A loser for a loser," Eleanor muttered as she stomped off to take her shower.

Leo scratched Magnolia between the ears. The dog looked up at him and seemed to grin.

"Think I could change her name, Mom?"

"She's probably used to it, Leo. You know the saying: you can't teach an old dog new tricks. But maybe if you could think of a name that sounds like Magnolia, then it wouldn't be such a change. Magnolia. Nola. Mango. Magnet. Magnificent."

"Maggie," Leo said. "Maggie! That would work. I like that name."

The dog wagged her tail.

"She knows that name, Mom, look. She knows it!" The dog came out from under the table and stretched in a long graceful bow. "Good girl, Maggie. You know your name, don't you, girl?"

For the first week after they brought Maggie home, the dog kept Leo or his mother in sight, following them from room to room. Outside, she was happy to lie in the grass with her head on her paws and wait while Leo played ball with Johnny or weeded the vegetable garden. Nothing seemed to bother her, not the fire engine's siren or the car alarm next door, not even Magoo, who liked to snack out of her food bowl. Nothing except Eleanor.

Maggie growled whenever Eleanor came into the room, a mini growl in the back of her throat. Sometimes Eleanor didn't hear it, but when she did, she complained. "I should be able to walk around in my own house without some has-been flea rug threatening me."

Sometimes Maggie barked at Eleanor with her ears flattened back and teeth showing. This was usually when Eleanor had wrapped her hair in a towel and painted her face with green beauty mud or when she was singing along to the music on her Walkman, her voice louder than she realized.

But one day Maggie bit Eleanor right above the ankle. Leo and Eleanor were fighting over the last little box of Crispo cereal.

"I asked Mom to buy it," Leo said.

"So what," Eleanor said, holding the box up over her head, just out of Leo's reach. "I got it."

Leo tried to jump and grab it. "It's mine. You know it, Eleanor. You never even heard of Crispo until I asked Mom for it."

"So what? I like it. I got it first. Back off, Dogboy. Eat a bone." Eleanor turned toward the cabinet to get a bowl. Leo lunged at her arm, and she dodged out of his way. Then Maggie entered the fight on Leo's side. She darted at Eleanor and nipped the back of her heel.

"*Ow!*" yelled Eleanor. She dropped the cereal and hopped up and down. "She bit me! I can't believe it. The dumb cur. MOM! The dog bit me. And there's foam at the corner of her mouth. HELP! She bit me and she's got rabies."

Eleanor's wails brought both her parents running. Mr. Nolan, in his underwear, with shaving cream covering half his face, reached the kitchen first. Leo was kneeling on the floor holding Maggie, who was licking his face. Eleanor was hopping around the room on one foot, holding her ankle and bellowing.

"Leo's vicious dog bit me. Look!" Eleanor displayed the back of her ankle.

"She doesn't look vicious to me," Mrs. Nolan said. She poured two cups of coffee while Mr. Nolan examined Eleanor's foot. "What were you doing to tease her?"

"Nothing!" Eleanor shrieked. "Nobody cares that she bit me, and in my own house."

"Of course we care, sweetheart," Mrs. Nolan said. "Sit down here and let's see that foot. Leo, get me some ice, please. It's not bleeding. And the dog is not foaming at the mouth. Calm down."

Eleanor collapsed at the table with an enormous sniff. She propped her leg up on a chair. Her father wrapped the ice cubes in a dish towel and arranged the bumpy bundle under Eleanor's ankle. The rest of the family sat down at the table, too.

"Nothing like a calm start to the day," Mr. Nolan said.

"Gets your blood running faster than coffee," Mrs. Nolan agreed.

Eleanor sniffed again to remind everyone that she had been injured. Leo kept quiet and stroked Maggie's back. What if his parents sent Maggie away? She wasn't vicious. He knew that. But they might believe Eleanor. Maggie didn't growl at anyone else.

"Somebody tell us what happened," Mr. Nolan said.

"I was just—" Eleanor began.

"She took my—" Leo started.

"Hold it. One at a time," their father said.

Eleanor described the scene, and Leo added a few details, like the way she had waved the box and made him jump around. Their parents listened, sipping coffee and nodding. Mr. Nolan put his hand to his mouth to cover a yawn and discovered the remains of his forgotten shaving cream.

"I have a pretty good idea what happened," Mrs. Nolan said. "Maggie is Leo's dog."

"I *know* that," Eleanor interrupted.

"Let me finish, please," her mother said. "Maggie's a smart dog, and she's made a strong bond with Leo. Seeing you with your arms raised and hearing you yell, Maggie probably thought that you were going to hurt Leo. So she raced in to protect him, which is just what a good dog does."

76

"Oh, swell," Eleanor said. "The mutt takes a hunk out of me and you say she's a good dog."

"A nip on the heel is hardly a hunk," Mr. Nolan pointed out. "You're both going to have to be careful about roughhousing. It's hard for dogs to know the difference between teasing and real danger."

Eleanor sulked, and Leo relaxed. His parents thought Maggie was a good dog. He wanted to give her a dog biscuit but then he realized that Eleanor might think he was rewarding Maggie for defending him. "Later," he whispered in her ear. She licked him right on the mouth.

"Yuck!" Eleanor groaned. "I can't watch this. It's disgusting. Dogboy and his faithful dog." She limped out of the room.

His mother sighed and his father shrugged. "She'll get over it. Just give her time," Mrs. Nolan said.

"Here Maggie, want a biscuit?" Mr. Nolan asked.

Maggie's ears came up a little, giving him an eager look. Then she sat up on her haunches and barked.

"Good dog," Leo said.

Escape

"Leee-ooo, oh Leee-ooo, I know you're up there. Help me come up. I want to come up there with you, Leee-ooo," the squeaky voice sing-songed.

Leo lay on his back as still as sleep. If he sat up his cousin Tim would know for sure that he'd tracked him down. His tree house was the one place Leo was safe. Tim couldn't climb up without Leo's help.

Ever since he'd arrived on Sunday afternoon, Tim had followed Leo like a shadow. He talked constantly, too, silly stuff about dinosaurs and Legos. By Sunday night Leo's head ached and he longed for some quiet privacy. But even after the light was turned off, Tim's high voice drowned out the crickets outside. Leo had never realized before how much he enjoyed listening to the crickets before falling asleep.

On Monday at breakfast, Leo complained to his mother. "Even the dog hides when she sees him coming."

"He's your cousin, Leo, and he loves you. You're his hero. He's only here for a week. Be nice to him. He's just a little boy."

"Mom! He whines all the time. He's worse than a mosquito."

"All little children whine. You were a champion whiner. Ask Eleanor," Mrs. Nolan said.

Eleanor looked up from her cereal and nodded hard. "'Mah-om, she hit me,'" Eleanor whined. "'Mah-om, she's using my crayons. She got the biggest piece. She won't let me play.' You whined so much, Leo, I wanted to take a piece of electric tape and seal your mouth shut."

"It's only for a week. You can put up with him for that long. You'll still have a month left before school." Mrs. Nolan refilled her coffee cup and started up the back stairs to her office. Leo sighed. The conversation was finished, he knew. He was stuck until Saturday. Maybe earplugs would work. He'd ask his mother to buy some. He tried to look on the bright side. After Tim left, there would still be time for pick-up baseball games, swimming, sleeping out in the tree house. Maybe even time to teach Maggie more tricks. He just might survive if he could get hold of earplugs.

Tim tagged along when Johnny and Leo went to the lake. Since he couldn't swim, he had to stay in the roped-off section where the lifeguards watched over the younger kids, giving Leo and Johnny some time to themselves out on the raft. Leo could see Tim waving from the kiddie section. The water was up to his armpits, and he waved his arms overhead, hoping to get Leo's attention.

"He acts like he's drowning," Johnny said, "but it's shallow in there."

"I wish he would drown," Leo said. "At least then he'd shut up."

Sure enough, as soon as they swam back to shore, Tim started talking, and he didn't let up all afternoon.

After dinner, Eleanor took Tim to the convenience store to get ice cream, another break for Leo. He rode his bike all alone in the twilight, trying to soak up the quiet.

But now it was Tuesday afternoon. All morning Tim had stuck by his side, yackety-yacking. The minute that Leo didn't do what Tim wanted, Tim's mouth screwed down, his eyebrows gathered into a frown, he wrinkled his nose, and the whine began. First the snuffle, sniff, sniff, snuffle. Then the beginning of an injured groan. He looked out of the corner of his eye to be sure that Leo's mother noticed. If not, then he moved closer and leaned against her, repeating the sniffle and groan and moving into the full whine. "Auntie Jane, Leo won't play with me." A few choked sobs, uhh—uhh—uhh. "It's not faaaa-ir. He's being meee-an." Then the crying, part whine, part howl.

What a fake, Leo thought. He rolled his eyes at his mother and put his palms together, begging for help. She winked and nodded, waving him away. "Come sit with me," she said to Tim, while Leo made his escape. That was half an hour ago. Thirty minutes peacefully reading comics in the tree house. But now the brat stood at the bottom of the tree making more noise.

Maybe I can lie here until dinner, Leo thought. I'll watch the leaves move and the clouds drift past the roof of the garage. He put his fingers in his ears but still he could hear Tim's voice.

"*Lee-oooo, Lee-oooo,* come down and get me, *Lee-oooo.* I want to come up. I've got candy, Leo. I'll share it with you."

Candy? It might be a trick, he thought. But Tim was too young to lie, wasn't he? If Leo sat up and looked over the edge, Tim would know that he was up here. Then he'd never go away, Leo thought. Still, if he had a big bag of good candy, something chewy, or if he had one of those giant, thick chocolate bars, it would be worth putting up with him.

"*Lee-oooo,* oh *Lee-oooo,* where are you, Leo?"

It sounded as if Tim was walking away, his voice getting fainter. Leo risked a peek. He could see the top of Leo's head with its cowlick bouncing as he walked. He couldn't see what he was holding in front of him. Did he have candy?

"Hey, Tim," he called. "Come back. I'll help you up."

The little boy trotted toward the tree with an adoring grin on his face. He gripped two lollipops in his grimy hand as if they were treasure. I lose, Leo thought.

"Here, Leo," Tim said, holding out one of the lollipops.

Leo climbed halfway down and jumped the rest of the distance. Tim handed over the candy. Inside its cellophane wrapper the lollipop was cracked into slivers.

"Put your foot on the wood and hold onto the top board," Leo instructed, hoisting his cousin up so he could reach the slat nailed to the trunk. "I'll hold you from the back. Don't be scared."

By stretching, Tim could just manage to reach the next slat with his foot. With a boost from Leo, Tim landed his stomach on the tree house floor and, like a seal pup, inched forward until he could pull his feet in and stand up.

"Neat!" he said. "It's so high. I'm a bird, Leo. Look. I'm a bird." He turned in circles, flapping his arms like wings.

"Be careful, buddy," Leo warned. "Don't go near the edge."

"What'll we play, Leo?" Tim asked.

Leo shrugged.

"Wanna play pirates?" Tim said. "This can be our ship. I'll be the captain, okay? We need hats and swords. Got any toys up here?"

"Nope. Just comics and stuff."

"What's in here?" Tim asked, shaking the metal treasure box. "Can I see?" Tim shook the box again and the contents rattled. "What's in here?"

"Arrowheads, old coins, a glass eye that Johnny got

from his uncle, some keys, my harmonica." Leo reached out to take the box, but Tim turned away, clutching it to his chest.

"I wanna see," Tim pouted. "I gave you candy. I'm gonna tell Aunt Jane on you."

Leo gritted his teeth. It was only Tuesday. He was stuck for another four days.

"You can't look in there. That's final. Hand it over. Right now." Leo tried to sound like a gangster in an old movie. "You don't want to know what will happen to you if you try opening that box."

Tim looked at him with wide eyes and handed back the metal box. His lower lip jutted out and began to quiver.

"How about cards?" Leo said quickly, trying to head off the wails he knew would come next.

"Go fish!" Tim said. "I go first."

Surprise, surprise, Leo thought. He dealt them each seven cards, set the deck between them on the floor, and arranged his hand. Two sixes and two nines. He set the pairs face down in front of him and drew four cards from the deck.

"Do you have any tens?" Tim asked.

"Go fish."

Tim picked up a card and frowned at his hand.

"Do you have any eights?" Leo asked. Reluctantly, Tim handed over the card.

That was the last card Leo got from his cousin. Every time after that, no matter what Leo asked for, Tim would say, "Go fish." Then mysteriously, in one or two more turns, Tim would ask for the same card from Leo and add another pair to his pile.

He's cheating, Leo thought. Five years old and he's cheating! Tim won the first game, and the second, and the third, every time smiling happily. Leo thought about challenging Tim to a game of old maid. It was impossible to cheat at old maid since it was all luck. But what would be the point? If Leo won, Tim would cry or pout or whine.

"This is fun, isn't it, Leo?" Tim said, gathering the cards up for another game.

Leo nodded dully, trying to think of a way to escape.

"I'm thirsty," Tim said. "Do you have any soda up here?"

This was the chance Leo needed. "I'll go get some for us. It won't take long. You can look at comics while I'm gone."

"Comics? I love comics. Do you have any Baby Huey?"

"Maybe a few. I'm not sure. They're in those milk crates in the corner. Be careful not to rip the pages, okay?"

"I'm not a baby. I'll be careful."

"I'll be back soon," Leo said. He climbed down the ladder and jogged toward the street, staying clear of the house. If his mother saw him, she'd be sure to ask, "Where's Tim?" And what could he tell her? Oh, I stashed him up in the tree house. He's afraid to climb down?

Leo headed for the corner store. He'd buy a small soda and they could split it. Maybe grape or root beer. Maybe lemon-lime. Not ginger ale. Leo hadn't liked that flavor when he was little because the bubbles made him sneeze.

In the field across from Murphy's Convenience Store, Leo spotted boys with gloves and bats, all wearing baseball caps. Johnny, Brian, Richard, Edward, and Ramon. They were choosing teams for a pick-up game. Leo could tell from the way they pointed, nodded, shook their heads. Five guys did not make two even teams, no matter how you tried to balance it out. The team with two players would always lose, even if the team at bat loaned them a catcher. Three on a side was the lowest you could go for a good game. That's why Leo wasn't surprised when they shouted as soon as they spotted him. "Hey, Leee-ooo! Wanna play?" Leo swung over the fence and ran to meet them.

"Hey-hey Leo, where've you been?" Edward asked.

"Taking care of my cousin."

"Want to play?" Brian asked. "We need a guy to make the sides even."

"I don't have my glove," Leo said. "And anyway, I've got to get back."

"We'll lend you a glove," Ramon said. "You gotta babysit?"

"Not exactly," Leo said.

"Then stay and play awhile," Richard said.

Leo knew he shouldn't stay. He glanced at Johnny, who nodded eagerly. "Okay," Leo said. "Just for a while."

The sides were matched, and both teams made slick plays, catching grounders and flies, hitting balls deep into center field. The game went three innings before a growl of thunder reminded Leo of the time. "How long have I been here?" Leo wailed to Johnny.

"I dunno. Maybe an hour. I don't have a watch."

Dark clouds piled up like boulders. Another peal of thunder crashed.

"It's gonna pour," Ramon warned. "Gimme my glove, Leo. I'm on my way."

Leo tossed the glove and waved good-bye to Johnny. "I gotta run, Ringer. Gotta get my cousin. Call you later." As he raced in the direction of the tree house, a flare of lightning flashed across the sky.

That's sheet lightning, Leo told himself, not the

kind that strikes. Or is it? Does thunder come with sheet lightning? Does lightning strike trees? Don't stand under trees in a thunderstorm, right?

Leo tried to imagine what Tim was doing right now. He's probably so scared he can't even cry. Maybe he tried to climb down and fell. He might be hurt, lying on the ground with a broken leg or a concussion.

Once when Leo had been about four years old, Eleanor brought him along when she went to her friend's house. The girls had gone inside to play, leaving Leo on the porch all by himself. A storm came up quickly, just like today, but the girls stayed inside. Leo huddled on the porch, frightened by the thunder and the windy rain. When lightning zigzagged across the sky, Leo rang the doorbell over and over, so scared he wet his pants. Eleanor finally opened the door and Leo socked her in the arm as hard as he could and screamed until she took him home.

He thought of this while running down the path to the tree house. Tim was only a little kid. It was a mean trick to strand him up in the tree house. Even before the storm came up, it was a nasty trick to play on a little kid.

I'll do something to make it up, Leo told himself. I'll give him all my old trucks. I'll get my castle out of the attic and let him play with it even though I never let anyone touch it, ever. I'll take him to the movies. I'll give him my Spiderman doll, the one Dad got for me in California. I'll let him eat my dessert every night until he goes home. He can pick the TV shows, too. He can even choose the cereal at the supermarket.

By the time Leo reached the tree, rain was pelting down in large drops, as hard as hail. Looking up at the tree house from the ground, Leo couldn't see Tim. He climbed up quickly. "Tim. *Tim*," he called. No answer. And no Tim. Where was he? No way could Tim manage to climb down the ladder. Maybe Leo's mother had heard Tim's wails and came to his rescue. If so, it meant big-time trouble for Leo. Hadn't she just told him to be nice to Tim?

Leo needed to get out from the rain and think for a minute. Don't panic, he told himself. Think. One corner of the tree house was sheltered by Johnny's grandfather's tent. Leo ducked under this and sat on the floor, chin on his hands, staring out at the rain. If he went home and Tim was there, he'd be in trouble for sure. If he went home and Tim wasn't there, he'd be in even more trouble. Still, he couldn't stay out here forever. Besides, if Tim was lost, everyone needed to help find him. That was the important thing—finding Tim.

By now the rain was flailing down in sheets, driven by the wind. Rain hit the tent so hard it sounded like the drummer in his father's favorite jazz group. Leo looked around the tree house for something to drape over his head as he ran to the house. Johnny's grandfather gave them two army blankets with the tent. Where were they? It was dark under the tent with storm clouds and the cover of the trees. Leo felt his way along the floor: milk crates, cookie tins, comics, a slingshot, a pail with a rope tied to the handle for hauling stuff up. Then, in the corner, his hands touched something soft and warm. Leo jumped back with a yelp. At the same moment, the lump said, "Leo?"

"Tim?"

"Where were you, Leo? I got sleepy. I found these blankets and made a nest. Like the birds. I took a nap. When did it start to rain? Where's my soda?"

Leo sat back on his heels. "Oh, Tim, you scared me. I couldn't find you."

"Where'd you think I was?" the little boy asked. He rubbed his eyes and stretched. "You told me to wait for you here. So that's what I did."

Leo hugged him and ruffled his hair. "Good boy," he said. Leo took a deep breath. Tim was safe. Whoa, that had been a close call. I am so lucky, Leo thought. Lucky, lucky, lucky.

He pulled Tim close beside him and draped an arm over his shoulder. The little boy was as warm as a puppy. Outside, the rain slowed to a gentle patter. The thunder and lightning stopped. Leo tickled Tim light-

ly in the ribs and made him squeal with pleasure. "Hey, Tim, why have just plain soda when we could have ice-cream sodas, right?"

"Right!" Tim hugged him back. "Can I get strawberry? I love strawberry. And I love you, Leo. You're the best cousin in the world."

I'm not but I will be, Leo vowed to himself. "Rain's just about stopped. Let's go, buddy," Leo said. "Strawberry soda coming up. My treat."